The Stray Dog

Retold and
illustrated
by

Marc
Simont

from
a true story
by Reiko Sassa

SCHOLASTIC INC.
New York Toronto London Auckland Sydney
Mexico City New Delhi Hong Kong Buenos Aires

ISBN 0-439-38591-1

12 11 10 9 8 7 6 5 4 3   2 3 4 5 6 7/0

Printed in the U.S.A.   24

First Scholastic printing, September 2002

Typography by Al Cetta

To Helen and Jenny

It was a great day for a picnic.

"What's this?" asked the father.

"It's a scruffy little dog," said the mother.

"He looks hungry," said the girl.

"I think he wants to play," said the boy.

The children played with him and taught him
to sit up. They named him Willy. They kept playing
until it was time to go.

"Let's take Willy home," said the children.

"No," said the father.

"He must belong to somebody," explained
the mother, "and they would miss him."

On the way home the girl said, "Maybe Willy
doesn't belong to anybody."

monday

During the week
all the family had
Willy on their minds.

tuesday

wednesday

thursday

friday

saturday

"Willy!" they all cried when he appeared.
But Willy didn't stop. Willy was in a big hurry.

"He has no collar. He has no leash," said the dog warden. "This dog is a stray. He doesn't belong to anybody."

The boy took off his belt.
"Here's his collar," he said.
The girl took off her hair
ribbon. "Here's his leash,"
she said. "His name is Willy,
and he belongs to us."

They took Willy home.

And after that . . .

they introduced him to the neighborhood,
where he met some very interesting dogs.

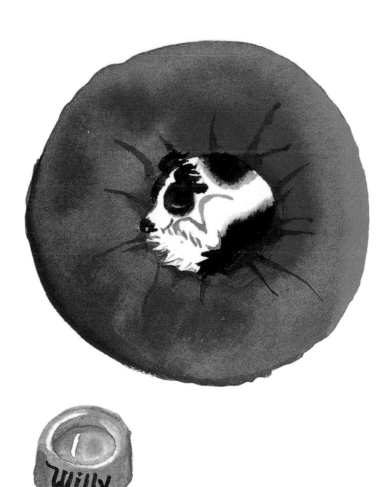

And Willy settled in where he belonged.